Katie Woo Has the Flu

by Fran Manushkin

illustrated by Tammie Lyon

PICTURE WINDOW BOOKS
a capstone imprint

Katie Woo is published by Picture Window Books,
a Capstone imprint
1710 Roe Crest Drive
North Mankato, Minnesota 56003
www.capstonepub.com

Text © 2012 Fran Manushkin
Illustrations © 2012 Picture Window Books

Library of Congress Cataloging-in-Publication Data
Manushkin, Fran.
 Katie Woo has the flu / by Fran Manushkin; illustrated by Tammie Lyon.
   p. cm. — (Katie Woo)
 Summary: Katie misses school while she is home with the flu.
ISBN 978-1-4048-6518-1 (library binding)
ISBN 978-1-4048-6854-0 (pbk.)
ISBN 978-1-4048-7661-3 (pbk.)
 [1. Sick—Fiction. 2. Influenza—Fiction. 3. Chinese Americans—Fiction.]
I. Lyon, Tammie, ill. II. Title.
 PZ7.M3195Kas 2011
 [E]—dc22   2011005488

Art Director: Kay Fraser
Graphic Designer: Emily Harris

Photo Credits
Fran Manushkin, pg. 26
Tammie Lyon, pg. 26

Printed in the United States of America in North Mankato, Minnesota.
092017   010743R

Table of Contents

Chapter 1

Ah-choo!

"Ah-choo!" said Katie Woo.

"Bless you!" said her mom.

"Ah-choo!" Katie sneezed

again and again and again.

"I feel funny," said Katie.
"But not in a fun way. My
tummy hurts, too."

"Uh-oh," said her mom.
"I think you have a bug."

"Ugh!" said Katie. "I don't want bugs running around in my tummy."

"Not that kind of bug," said her mom. "A flu bug."

"Good," said Katie. "But I still feel bad."

"I feel hot, too," Katie moaned. Her mom took her temperature.

"You have a fever," she said. "That's why you feel so hot. No school today! You are going back to bed."

"I feel so hot, I might melt!"

Katie moaned.

"Don't worry," her mom
assured her. "You're not ice
cream. You won't melt."

"I'm so glad!" said Katie.

Chapter 2

Sick at Home

Soon Katie began to shiver. "How can I feel cold and hot at the same time?" she wondered.

"The flu is tricky," said her mom.

"That's a sneaky trick," said Katie.

Katie's mom gave her pills to take. "Yuck," Katie groaned. "Pills are such . . . pills."

Katie fell asleep and had

a bad dream. She dreamed

she was a polar bear who

lost her fur. She shivered and

shook!

When Katie woke up,
her mom read her a story. It
was about a girl with hair so
long, she could jump rope
with it.

Her dad sang her a happy

song.

Katie drew a picture of the

flu bug flying away from her.

Katie's mom brought her

hot soup and toast.

"Ew, soup!" Katie moaned.

"Ew, toast! I'm not hungry."

Later, JoJo called Katie.

"I missed you today! Miss

Winkle says it's not the same

without you."

"Thanks," Katie croaked.

"Ribbit!" JoJo croaked

back. Katie smiled.

Then Pedro
called. He told Katie,
"When I broke my
leg, everyone wrote
funny things on my
cast."

"Lucky you,"
said Katie.
"There is no cast
with the flu."

She drew a picture of everyone writing their names on her arms.

"That would tickle," Katie decided.

Chapter 3

Feeling Better

Katie took another little nap. When she woke up, she felt a lot better.

Her mom brought her

more soup and toast.

"Yay, soup!" Katie said.

"Yay, toast! I'm starving!"

"I'm feeling more like me," Katie said. "It feels good to feel good!"

That night, Katie dreamed that her class sang a "Welcome Back" song to her.

Miss Winkle played the tambourine and did a happy dance.

A few days later, Katie went back to school. Her friends welcomed her with a song.

"Boo on the flu," they sang. "We missed you!"

"I did too!" sang Miss Winkle.

Katie sang back: "I feel like new! Like a new Katie Woo!"

And it was true!

About the Author

Fran Manushkin is the author of many
popular picture books, including *How Mama
Brought the Spring; Baby, Come Out!; Latkes
and Applesauce: A Hanukkah Story;* and *The
Tushy Book*. There is a real Katie Woo — she's
Fran's great-niece — but she never gets in
half the trouble of the Katie Woo in the books.
Fran writes on her beloved Mac computer in New York City,
without the help of her two naughty cats, Miss Chippie
and Goldy.

About the Illustrator

Tammie Lyon began her love for drawing
at a young age while sitting at the
kitchen table with her dad. She continued
her love of art and eventually attended
the Columbus College of Art and Design,
where she earned a bachelors degree in fine
art. After a brief career as a professional
ballet dancer, she decided to devote herself full time to
illustration. Today she lives with her husband, Lee, in Cincinnati,
Ohio. Her dogs, Gus and Dudley, keep her company as she works
in her studio.

Glossary

assured (uh-SHURD)—promised something

croaked (KROHKD)—spoke in a deep hoarse voice

fever (FEE-ver)—a body temperature that is higher than normal

groaned (GROHND)—made a long, low sound showing that someone is in pain

moaned (MOHND)—made a low, sad sound

tambourine (tam-bur-EEN)—a small, round musical instrument that is similar to a drum. It has jingling metal disks around the rim and is played by shaking or striking it with the hand.

temperature (TEM-pur-uh-chur)—the degree of heat or cold in something, usually measured by a thermometer

Discussion Questions

1. What were the signs that Katie was sick?

2. What is the worst part about being sick? Are there any good parts?

3. Katie's mom brought her soup and toast to eat. What foods do you eat when you are sick?

Writing Prompts

1. Make a get-well card for Katie. Write her a special note.

2. Write a story about a time when you were sick. How did you feel? How long were you sick? What made you feel better?

3. Katie dreamed that she was a bear that lost all its fur. Write a story about a bear that has no hair.

In *Katie Woo Has the Flu*, Katie thought she had bugs running around in her tummy! If you eat this great treat, you could have bugs in your tummy, too.

Bugs on a Log

What you need:

- a butter knife
- 2 celery stalks, cut in half
- 1/3 cup peanut butter
- 1/4 cup raisins

What you do:

1. Using the butter knife, fill the hollows of the celery with peanut butter.

2. Place raisins (or bugs) on the peanut butter.

3. Enjoy!

Become a chef and experiment with different ingredients. Here are some ideas you can mix and match.

Instead of peanut butter, use . . .
- cream cheese
- cheese spread
- hummus
- tuna salad
- tofu dip

Instead of raisins, use . . .
- chocolate chips
- marshmallows
- sunflower seeds
- peanuts
- pine nuts
- diced carrots
- currants

THE FUN DOESN'T STOP HERE!

Discover more at www.capstonekids.com

- Videos & Contests
- Games & Puzzles
- Friends & Favorites
- Authors & Illustrators

Find cool websites and more books like this one at www.facthound.com. Just type in the Book ID: **9781404865181** and you're ready to go!

Hi! I'm Katie Woo.

My mom says that I have a bug.
I thought that meant there is a
bug running around in my tummy.
But it just means I am sick. Now
I have to stay home from school
and eat boring things like soup
and toast. Why won't this flu bug
just go away?

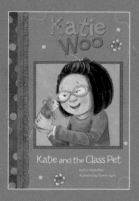

Katie and the Class Pet

Katie Woo,
Where Are You?

Katie's New Shoes

005-007 RL: 1.5 GRL: H

ISBN 978-1-4048-6854-0

PICTURE WINDOW BOOKS™
a capstone imprint www.capstonepub.com

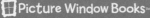